W9-CIP-521

Start-Off StorieS

THE ANT AND THE DOVE

An Aesop Tale Retold

By Mary Lewis Wang

Illustrated by Ching

Prepared under the direction of Robert Hillerich, Ph.D.

CHILDRENS PRESS®

CHICAGO

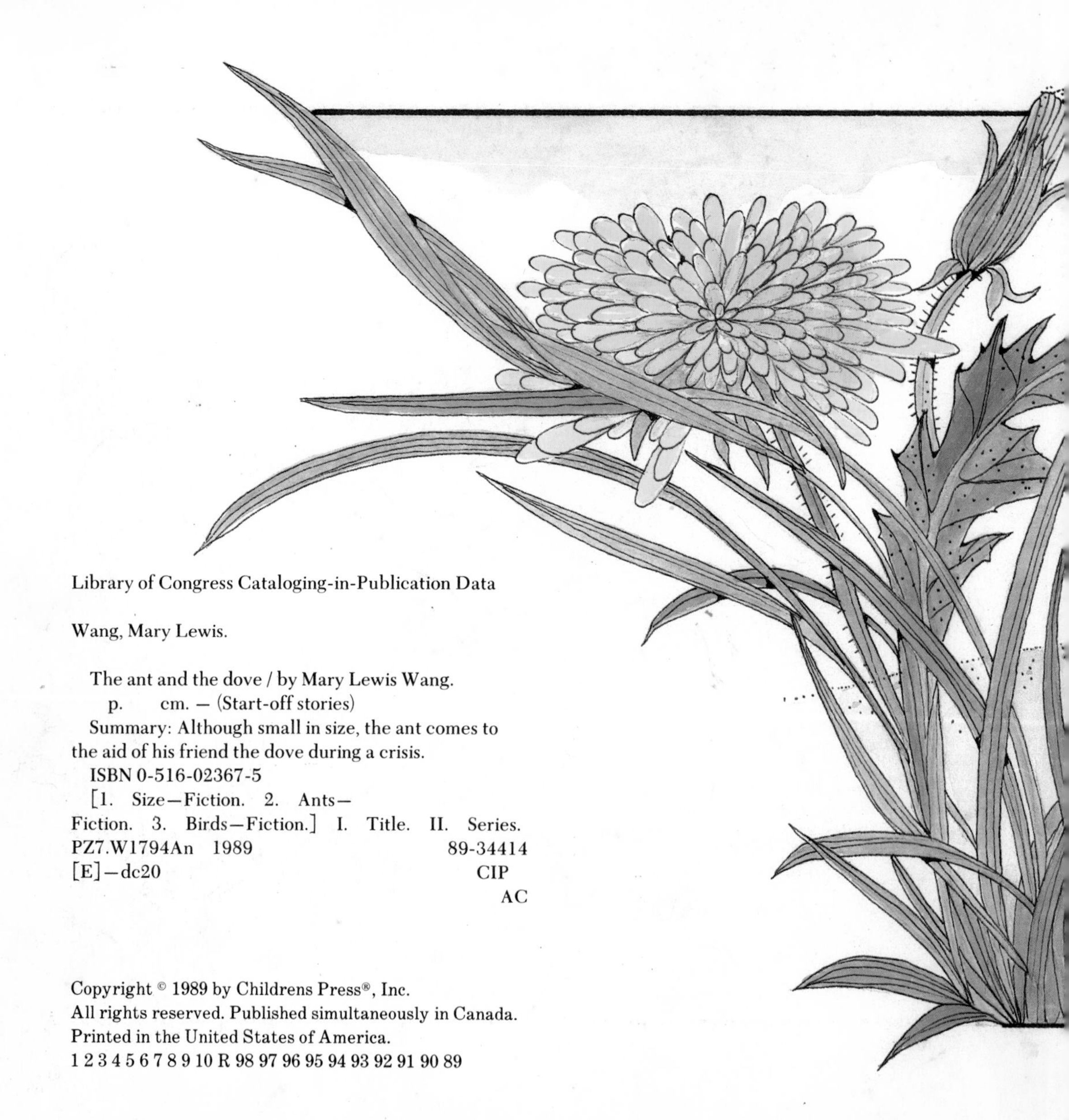

Library of Congress Cataloging-in-Publication Data

Wang, Mary Lewis.

The ant and the dove / by Mary Lewis Wang.
p. cm. — (Start-off stories)
Summary: Although small in size, the ant comes to the aid of his friend the dove during a crisis.
ISBN 0-516-02367-5
[1. Size—Fiction. 2. Ants—Fiction. 3. Birds—Fiction.] I. Title. II. Series.
PZ7.W1794An 1989 89-34414
[E]—dc20 CIP
AC

Printed in the United States of America.
1 2 3 4 5 6 7 8 9 10 R 98 97 96 95 94 93 92 91 90 89

A little ant was thirsty.
He ran out to get
some water.

But when he came
to the water,
he fell in.

“Help!” said the ant.
“Help! Help!”

A dove saw the ant.
in the water.
The dove said, “Coo.
I know what to do.”

The dove went to get
a leaf.

She let the leaf
fall to the water.
It came down next to
the ant.

So the happy ant
had a ride.

“Thank you, good dove,”
said the ant.
“You did a good deed.
Someday I will do
something for you.”

The dove said, “Coo.
What could an ant do?”

Just then the ant saw
a man with a net.
The man was about to
net the good dove.

"I can do this,"
said the ant.
The little ant ran to the man.
He ran, ran, ran.

Then he bit the man.

"Ouch!" said the man.
Down came the net.
Up went the dove.

The dove said, “Coo.
Little ant, thank you.”

The ant said,
"An ant can do
a good deed, too."

WORD LIST

a
about
an
ant
bit
but
came
can
coo
could
deed
did
do
dove
down
fall
fell
for
get
good
had
happy
he
help
I
in
it
just
know
leaf
let
little
man
net
next
ouch
out
ran
ride
said
saw
she
so
some
someday
something
thank
the
then
thirsty
this
to
too
up
was
water
went
what
when
will
with
you

About the Author

Mary Lewis Wang is the author of three other Start-Off Stories: *The Lion and the Mouse*, *The Frog Prince*, and *The Good Witch*. She also has edited many books for both children and adults as an editor with McGraw-Hill, Golden Books (Western Publishing Co.), and John Wiley & Sons. A native New Yorker, she is now a resident of St. Louis, Missouri. She and her husband are the parents of three grown children.

About the Artist

Mary "Ching" Walters has twenty-three years of experience as a free-lance artist with primary concentration in the area of postage-stamp design, wildlife paintings, and illustrations for many greeting card companies. She has illustrated several children's books. Originally from Tennessee, Ching currently lives in St. Louis, Missouri with her husband Bob, a TWA pilot, and their dog Sandy.